W9-CFC-696

POLLY THE PERSNICKETY PACHYDERM,
Copyright © 1999 by Lena Herlihy for Woods in the Round, LLC
All rights reserved. No part of this book may be reproduced or transmitted in any form or by any means, electronic or mechanical, including photocopying, recording or by any information storage or retrieval system, without permission in writing from the publisher, except a reviewer who may reproduce illustrations and quote passages of text in a review. For information, address Woods-in-the-Round Publishing
PO Box 5364, Niceville, Florida 32578

Book designed and edited by Sandy Meyer

https://www.etsy.com/shop/WoodsintheRound

Library of Congress Cataloging-in-Publication Data
Lena Herlihy
    Polly the Persnickety Pachyderm / Lena Herlihy. - 1st ed.
        p.   cm
    ISBN-13: 978-1518797590
    ISBN-10: 1518797598
    1. Title.

FIRST EDITION

10 9 8 7 6 5 4 3 2 1

Polly the Persnickety Pachyderm

by
Lena Herlihy
&
Sandy Meyer

Illustrated by Candace Thieme

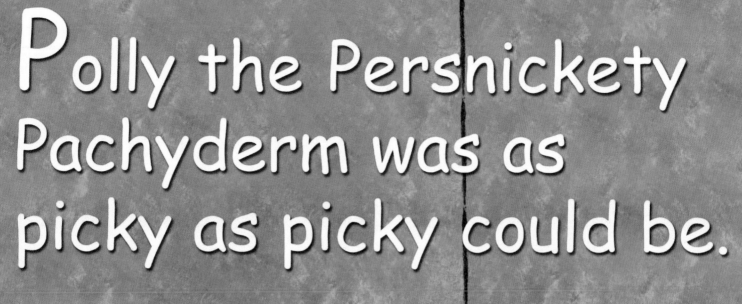

Polly the Persnickety Pachyderm was as picky as picky could be.

She only ate foods from one food group, those foods beginning with "P".

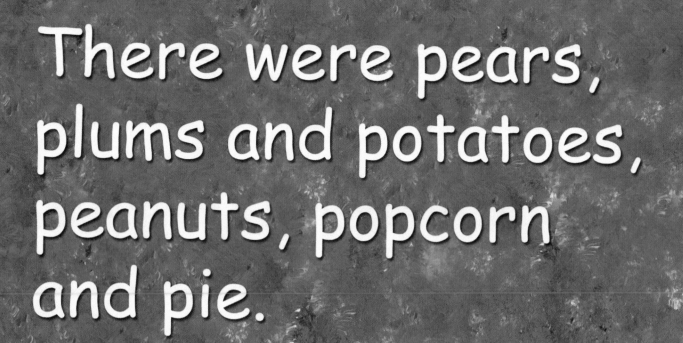

There were pears,
plums and potatoes,
peanuts, popcorn
and pie.

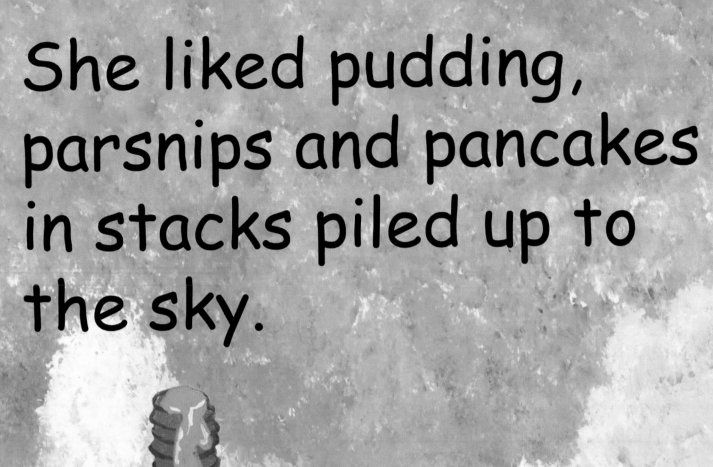

She liked pudding, parsnips and pancakes in stacks piled up to the sky.

Polly was fond of pineapples and

pumpkin pureed with
pure spice.

Pralines with plump pecans in them, Polly found particularly nice.

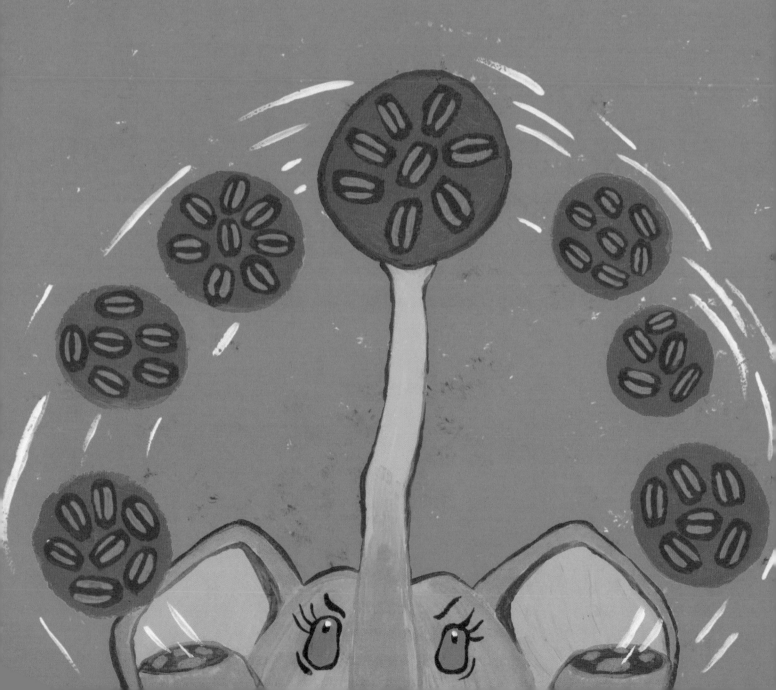

Peaches pleased Polly profusely,

and pasta sure made Polly smile.

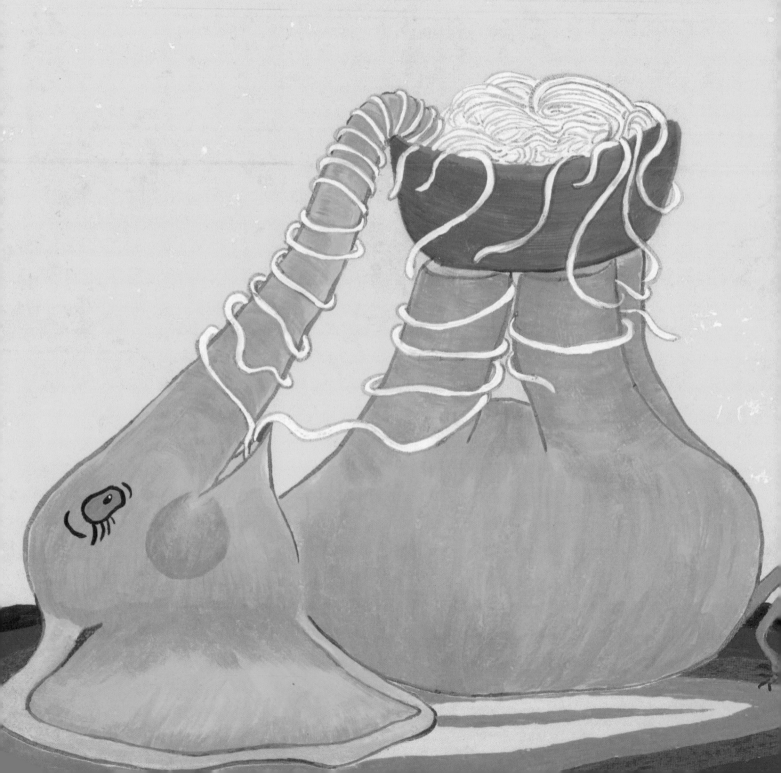

For a slice, maybe
two, of hot pizza,

Polly would run
for a mile.

One day while Polly was partaking from a pot of piping hot peas,

Polly spotted a green bean half-eaten

and Polly got weak at the knees!

"I've eaten a bean!" fretted Polly,

Then another bite and Polly pondered, "You know, this bean isn't half bad!"

So now Polly has a
new menu,

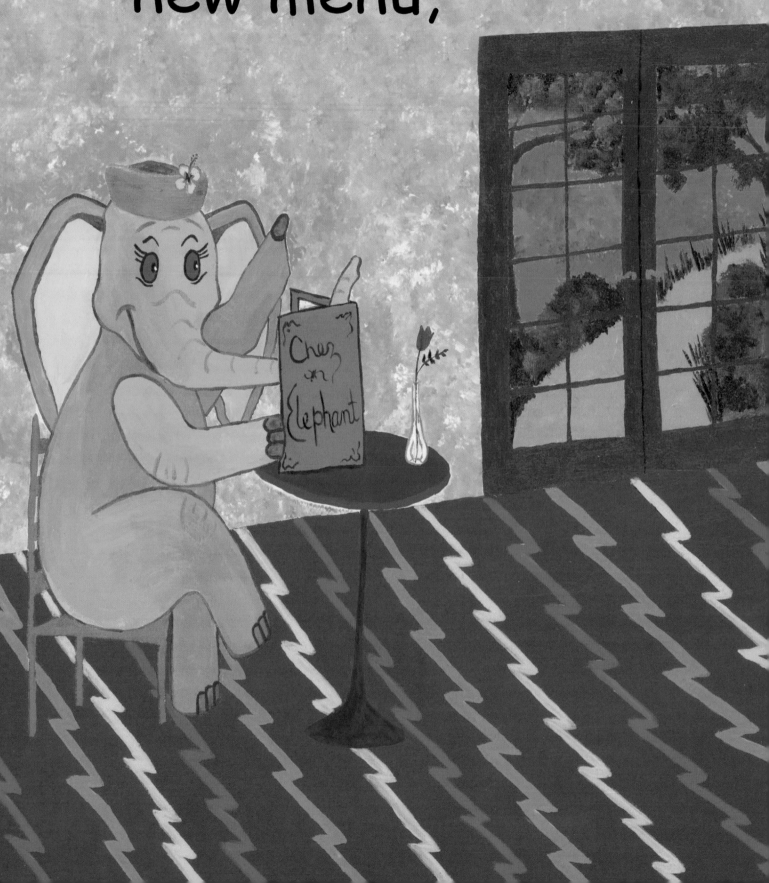

one expanding the things she can get

And starting today,
she's having an " A "

and then the <u>rest</u> of the alphabet!

Look back through the book and see what foods you'll find from "A" to "Z"!

68397609R00020

Made in the USA
Charleston, SC
08 March 2017